Annie and Snowball and the Cozy Nest

The Fifth Book of Their Adventures

Cynthia Rylant
Illustrated by Suçie Stevenson

READY-TO-READ

ALADDIN

New York   London   Toronto   Sydney

For my good friends:
Sarah Robinson, Lisa Markley, and Sophie
—S. S.

ALADDIN
An imprint of Simon & Schuster Children's Publishing Division
1230 Avenue of the Americas, New York, NY 10020
First Aladdin paperback edition March 2010
ALADDIN is a trademark of Simon & Schuster, Inc.,
and related logo is a registered trademark of Simon & Schuster, Inc.
READY-TO-READ is a registered trademark of Simon & Schuster, Inc.
Also available in a Simon & Schuster Books for Young Readers
hardcover edition.
For information about special discounts for bulk purchases,
please contact Simon & Schuster Special Sales at 1-866-506-1949
or business@simonandschuster.com.
The Simon & Schuster Speakers Bureau can bring authors
to your live event. For more information or to book an event contact
the Simon & Schuster Speakers Bureau at 1-866-248-3049
or visit our website at www.simonspeakers.com.
Designed by Tom Daly
The text of this book was set in Goudy Old Style.
The illustrations for this book were rendered in pen-and-ink and watercolor.
Manufactured in the United States of America
0110 LAK
2 4 6 8 10 9 7 5 3 1
The Library of Congress has cataloged the hardcover edition as follows:
Rylant, Cynthia.
Annie and Snowball and the cozy nest / Cynthia Rylant;
Illustrated by Suçie Stevenson—1st ed.
p. cm.
Summary: Annie and her bunny watch and wait as a nest is built above the porch
swing, and eventually they get to see the mother bird feeding her babies.
ISBN 978-1-4169-3943-6 (hc)
[1. Nests—Fiction. 2. Birds—Fiction. 3. Animals—Infancy—Fiction.]
I. Stevenson, Suçie, ill. II. Title.
PZ7.R982 Anc 2009
[E]—dc22
2007031056
ISBN 978-1-4169-3947-4 (pbk)

Contents

Happy Day

It was May and Annie was happy.

So many good things were happening.

Her cousin, Henry, was having a birthday.

The tulips she planted were blooming.
And on her porch someone
was making a nest.
The nest was in a safe little spot.

6

Annie had seen it one day
when she was reading
with her bunny, Snowball.
"Snowball, look!" Annie had said.
"A nest!"

Annie called Henry next door and
asked him to come and see the nest.
He did.

And every day since then
Annie and Henry had hoped to see
who was building the nest.

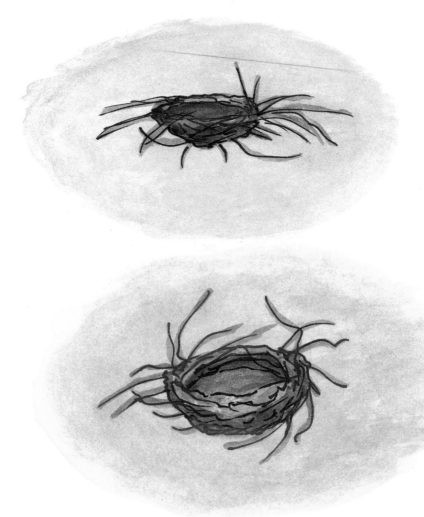

The nest was getting bigger and bigger.

Annie could see the bits of twig and
bits of leaves and even some small bits
of fur.

She wondered if it was Snowball fur.
Then she wondered if it was Mudge fur.

Henry's big dog, Mudge, had enough
extra fur to fill an elephant's nest!
(If elephants built nests.)

Annie checked the little nest
every day to see if anyone was home.
But so far no one had moved in.

A New Neighbor

One day Annie was reading
on the swing when a little robin
swooped above her head.
The swoop made Snowball jump.

15

Annie looked up at the nest.
Someone was home!
It was the little robin!

Annie watched quietly as the little
robin settled into her cozy home.
The nest was in a perfect place to
hatch babies.

A person would never know the nest was there unless he sat on Annie's swing.

And no one sat on Annie's swing except Annie and Snowball and sometimes Henry and sometimes Annie's dad.

Mudge did not sit on Annie's swing.
(Though sometimes he tried.)

The little robin and the little nest
were perfectly safe.
Annie had a new neighbor!

Waiting and Waiting

For days and days Annie quietly watched
the little robin sit in its cozy nest.
The little bird was almost always there.

When it flew away, Annie worried that
it might not come back.
But it always did.
And Annie knew why.

One day when the bird was away, Annie's
dad lifted her up to look inside the nest.

"Five eggs!" whispered Annie.
"Five blue eggs!"

Annie's dad told her she could look at the eggs but not to touch them.

He said that mother birds do not like fingers touching their eggs.
So Annie did not touch.

She wanted the little robin to be happy
living on the porch.
Henry and his dad came over to see
the eggs too.

"Five eggs," said Henry's dad. "She's
hatching a basketball team."

Annie and Henry laughed.

Henry's dad could be so silly.

Everyone could hardly wait to see the

babies.

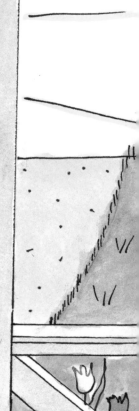

A Family

The baby birds picked the perfect
morning to hatch.
It was a Saturday morning.

Annie and Annie's dad and Henry
and Henry's dad and Henry's mom
and Snowball and Mudge were all
in Annie's kitchen having pancakes.

(Snowball loved lettuce pancakes.)

The doors were open. The windows were open.

And somehow everyone was chewing at the same time, so it was quiet.

Then suddenly . . . *cheep cheep cheep cheep cheep*!

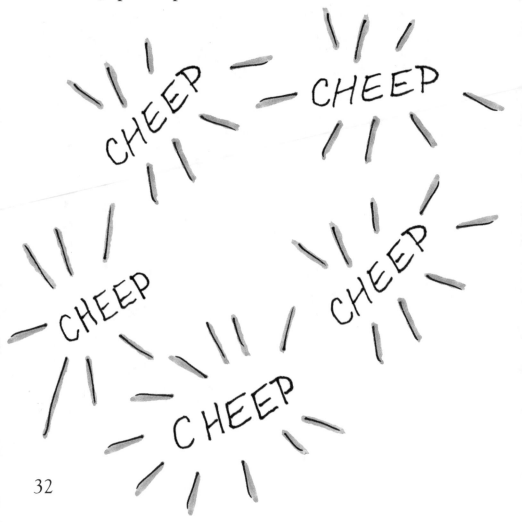

The sounds came from the front porch!
And they were loud!

Annie's dad said, "I think someone else
wants breakfast!"
Everyone hurried to the porch.

And there in the cozy nest were five
baby birds, eyes closed, mouths open,
all cheeping.

The little robin was perched on the
nest, putting bits of food in each
baby's mouth.
"They're beautiful!" said Annie.
"And really hungry!" said Henry.

Mudge's ears were perked up.
Cheeping was a new sound to him.

"I'm proud of the mother," said Annie.
"She waited and waited and waited."
When the last baby was fed, the little
robin flew off to find more food.

37

"That reminds me," said Henry.

"Pancakes!" said Henry and Annie together.

They all went back inside to the table.
Then everyone was chewing *and* talking.
It had been an exciting morning.
The excitement had made them hungrier.

While everyone ate, Mudge and
Snowball curled up under the table.

"Look," said Annie. "Snowball has her own cozy nest."
"Yes," said Henry, "but this nest snores!"

I call it the pig paddle, thought Fluffy.

"Just look at him go!" said Wade.

Zoe and the Aqua Girls ran over.

"Is Fluffy doing the crawl?" said Zoe.

"Not really," said Wade.

"Is he doing the dog paddle?" said Zoe.

"Not exactly," said Maxwell.

"Then what *is* he doing?" said Zoe.

Fluffy kept his head up.

He kept his feet on the sand.

He began to trot through the water.

"Look, Zoe!" called Maxwell.

"Fluffy learned to swim!"

The boys took Fluffy back
into the lake.
They put him down
in very shallow water.
Fluffy's paws touched the sand.
Here comes Aqua Pig! thought
Fluffy.

Aqua Pig bobbed up again.

He heard the crowd cheering,

"Fluffy! Fluffy! Fluffy!"

Aqua Pig opened his eyes.

"Fluffy! Fluffy!" Wade was saying.

"Wake up. You were dreaming."

Aqua Pig floated on his back.
He put both hind feet up in the air.
He reached up with his front paws
and touched his toes.
Aqua Pig sank slowly into the lake.
"Hooray for Aqua Pig!" yelled the crowd.

Aqua Pig turned over onto his back.
He put one hind leg up in the air.
He pointed his toes.
"Bravo!" shouted the fans.

The fans clapped and cheered
as Aqua Pig paddled out into the lake.
He put his face in the water.
He blew bubbles through his nose.
He moved his arms and kicked.
"Yay!" called the fans.

I wish I could be in a big water show,
thought Fluffy. He closed his eyes.
"Most guinea pigs don't swim,"
said the announcer.
"But there is one who does.
Put your hands together
for the one and only . . . Aqua Pig!"

The Aqua Girls floated on their backs.
They put both feet up in the air.
They reached up with their hands
and touched their toes.
They sank slowly into the lake.
Then they bobbed up again.
Cool, thought Fluffy.

Fluffy watched the Aqua Girls
swim out into the lake.
They turned over onto their backs.
They each put one leg up in the air.
They pointed their toes.
Wow! thought Fluffy.

Zoe and her friends came by.
They patted Fluffy and fed him a carrot.
"We are the Aqua Girls," Zoe told Fluffy.
"We are going to be in a big water show.
Watch what we do."

Aqua Pig!

The boys put Fluffy down on the dock.

"See you later, Fluffy!" they said.

Then they jumped into the lake and

swam off.

Maxwell took his hand away.

Fluffy started to sink.

Maxwell picked him up.

"I guess guinea pigs don't swim,"
Wade said.

Right! thought Fluffy.

Pigs don't swim!

"Fluffy can't do the crawl like we do,"
said Maxwell. "But maybe
he can paddle like a dog."
Maxwell held Fluffy under his tummy.
"Paddle with your paws," he said.
Fluffy paddled.
Now what? he thought.

Fluffy put his face in the water.
He tried to blow bubbles through
his nose.
He tried to move his arms and kick.
But he came up sputtering.

Wade and Maxwell carried Fluffy back
into the lake.
"This is how I do the crawl," Wade said.
"I put my face in the water.
I blow bubbles through my nose."
Through your *nose*? thought Fluffy.
"Then I move my arms and kick," said Wade.

"That was a close one," said Wade.

"You know what we have to do?"
said Maxwell.

"We have to teach Fluffy to swim."

No way! thought Fluffy.

Wade and Maxwell carried Fluffy
back to his cage.
They fed him an apple.
They scratched him behind the ears.
Ahhh! thought Fluffy.
A pig could get used to this.

Just then Wade and Maxwell
ran over.

"That's our guinea pig!" said Wade.

The girl gave Fluffy to him.

"Fluffy!" said Wade. "You're alive!"

"Thank you for saving him,"
Maxwell told the girl.

"Bye, Fishy!" said the girl.

The Swimming Lesson

The girl and her father
took Fluffy out of the water wing.
They dried him off with a towel.
"Can I keep him?" said the girl.
"I will call him Fishy."
Fishy? thought Fluffy.
I don't think so.

Suddenly, something yanked Fluffy
out of the water.
The next thing he knew,
a girl with a fishing pole
was staring at him.
He was swinging
on the end of her fishing line.
Nice catch! thought Fluffy.

Just then, a hook caught the water wing.

Fluffy heard a hissing sound.

Air was leaking out!

I am a sinking pig! thought Fluffy.

HELP! HELP! HELP!

A boat roared by. It made big waves.

The waves bounced Fluffy around.

He was getting dizzy.

Glug! thought Fluffy.

Somebody help this pig!

A dog paddled by.
Nice doggy, thought Fluffy.
A fish leapt out of the lake.
Down, fish! thought Fluffy.

"Oh, no!" said Maxwell.

"Hold on, Fluffy!" called Wade.

"We will save you!"

When? thought Fluffy.

How about NOW?

A puff of wind blew Fluffy
across the lake.
When the boys looked back,
Fluffy was far away.

The boys put Fluffy in the water.

Fluffy bobbed up and down.

"Go, Fluffy!" said Maxwell and Wade.

Uh-oh! thought Fluffy.

The boys turned toward the shore.

"Zoe! Charlotte! Look!" called Maxwell.

"Fluffy is swimming!" called Wade.

Maxwell stopped blowing and
tucked in the plug.
The boys carried Fluffy into the lake.
"Now you can swim, Fluffy!" Wade said.
One little problem, thought Fluffy.
Pigs don't swim!

Wade put Fluffy into the middle
of the water wing.
Maxwell blew it up.
Fluffy felt the ring get tight.
I feel like a hot dog in a bun!
thought Fluffy.

Zoe took Charlotte into the lake.

Wade picked up a yellow water wing.

He looked at the water wing.

He looked at Fluffy.

Don't even think about it,

thought Fluffy.

"What are those?" asked Maxwell.

"Water wings," said Zoe.

"They help Charlotte keep her head above water. But Charlotte can't go into the lake alone because she can't swim yet."

Just like me, thought Fluffy.

The boys carried Fluffy's cage
down to the lake.
Wade's Mom was already there.
So was his big sister, Zoe,
and his little sister, Charlotte.
Zoe had some plastic rings.
She slid them onto Charlotte's arms
and blew them up.

Everyone ran into the lake house
to put on a swimsuit.
"Too bad you don't have
a swimsuit, Fluffy," said Wade.
I don't need one, thought Fluffy.
Pigs don't swim.

"We can swim in the lake all day,"
said Wade.

"Hot dog!" said Maxwell.

"Can Fluffy go swimming, too?"

"He can't swim," said Wade.

Right! thought Fluffy. **Pigs don't swim.**

Guinea Pigs Don't Swim

Wade's family drove to their lake house.

Wade asked Maxwell to come along.

The boys brought Fluffy, too.